THE CASE OF THE MYSTERY CRUISE™

A novelization by Carol Thompson

DUALSTAR PUBLICATIONS

PARACHUTE PRESS, INC.

SCHOLASTIC INC.

New York Toronto London Auckland Sydney

DUALSTAR PUBLICATIONS

PARACHUTE PRESS, INC.

Dualstar Publications
c/o 1801 Century Park East
Los Angeles, CA 90067

Parachute Press, Inc.
156 Fifth Avenue
Suite 325
New York, NY 10010

Published by Scholastic Inc.

With special thanks to Robert Thorne and Harold Weitzberg.

Printed in the U.S.A.
April 1996
ISBN: 0-590-86370-3
H I J

Ready for Adventure?

It was the best of times. It was the worst of times. Actually it was bedtime when our great-grandmother would read us stories of mystery and suspense. It was then that we decided to be detectives.

The story you are about to read is one of the cases from the files of the Olsen & Olsen Agency. We call it *The Case of the Mystery Cruise*.

Our family was taking a trip on an ocean cruise ship. It was supposed to be a vacation. But a ship is a great place for high adventure on the high seas!

Before we knew it, someone had stolen Dad's top-secret computer disk. And now the thief was after us! It was a case only the Trenchcoat Twins could crack.

No matter what, we always live up to our motto: Will Solve Any Crime By Dinner Time!

Chapter 1

"Hey, Ashley," I whispered. "There's a sneaky-looking character." I pointed across the deck of the ship. "Check out that little hairy guy in the green chair."

Ashley took a closer look. "Mary-Kate!" she cried. "That's not a guy. That's a poodle!"

"I know! But look at the lady sitting *next* to the poodle," I said. "The one in the pink sundress. *She* looks sneaky. She has very shifty eyes."

Ashley groaned. "Mary-Kate, you're trying too hard to find a mystery."

"Maybe I am." I sighed and pulled down the brim of my blue baseball cap.

No crime in sight? That's bad news for two super-duper snoopers.

My name is Mary-Kate Olsen. My twin sister, Ashley, and I are the Trenchcoat Twins. What do we do? We solve crimes. We *love* mysteries! We're detectives!

We usually work in our detective office. It's in the attic of our house in California. And usually our big brother, Trent, gives us a really hard time. Trent is eleven. He always makes fun of our detective work.

Lizzie, our six-year-old sister, is totally different. And even worse. Because Lizzie loves our detective agency. She's always following us around and getting in the way.

But right now we didn't have to worry about Lizzie or Trent. Lizzie was visiting our great-grandma Olive. (Great-grandma Olive is the one who got Ashley and me started as detectives. But more about that later.)

And Trent was away at summer camp.

Ashley and I were on a really cool cruise ship—on vacation with our parents.

The ship is great. It's like a big summer camp floating on the ocean. It has two swimming pools, a theater, and two game rooms—one for adults and one just for kids.

Sounds like fun, right?

Wrong!

Because Ashley and I think that solving mysteries is the most fun of all. And there were no mysteries on board this ship.

"So far this vacation is the *pits,*" I told Ashley. "I'm tired of checking out the people by the pool. The only case we'll find around here is a bad case of sunburn! Come on, let's try the game room."

"Wait one minute." Ashley picked up her purple marker and went back to work on the sign she was making.

I stared at my sister. Sometimes it's hard to believe that we're twins. We're both nine years old. We both have strawberry blond hair and big blue eyes. We both look exactly alike.

But we sure don't act alike. Or think alike!

Ashley likes to take her time with everything. She thinks and thinks about every problem. And then she thinks some more. She studies every possible clue before she makes a move. Then when she does move, it's very, very slowly.

Not me. I always want to jump right in!

Ashley put down her marker and held up the sign. "How does this look?" she asked.

"Upside down," I said. But I could still read what it said:

OLSEN & OLSEN
MYSTERY AGENCY
SHIPBOARD OFFICE
VERANDA DECK, ROOM 42
WILL SOLVE ANY CRIME BY DINNER TIME

Yes! I slapped Ashley a high five. "Now

everyone on the ship will know there are two detectives around."

"And soon we'll have more cases than we can handle!" Ashley said.

I rubbed my hands together in excitement. "Mysteries, here we come!" I cheered.

"Calm down," Ashley told me. "You always get so excited. Be sensible. This sign might help us find a case. But it might not."

"Let's *not* be sensible right now," I said. "Let's just hang up this sign and see what happens. The only question is, where?"

Ashley pushed back her chair. "Why, we'll hang it on the ship's bulletin board, of course," she said. "That's only—"

"Logical!" I shouted the word, before Ashley could say it.

It's not that Ashley is wrong. Detectives *should* be calm and logical—sometimes. But it was hard to be calm—I had a hunch we were about to stumble onto a big case.

I followed Ashley across the open deck. (A deck is what you call the floor on a ship.) We stopped at the bulletin board. Ashley began to tack up the sign.

I crammed my hands into my pockets. I felt a stack of small paper cards. Our business cards!

"Hey, Ashley. While you do that, I'll hand out these cards we made." The business cards said that we were detectives. And told people where to find us. Ashley and I had made them our first night on this cruise. I had forgotten all about them!

"These cards should bring in plenty of business," I said.

I started handing out cards to the people passing by.

"Detectives for hire!" I shouted. "Call the Trenchcoat Twins! The ones to choose when you're on a cruise!"

Nobody paid any attention.

I tried again. "Hire Mary-Kate and Ashley! Two detectives for the price of one!"

Nobody seemed at all interested.

Ashley straightened her pink headband. She smoothed her pink and white skirt. She turned to the next group of passengers walking by and flashed them her brightest smile.

"Don't let crime spoil vacation time!" Ashley said.

The passengers kept on walking.

"These people don't have any mysteries to solve right now." Ashley shrugged. "There's nothing we can do. We'll just have to wait for a crime to happen."

"But we can't wait!" I cried. "We have to do something. And fast!"

Ashley looked at me closely. "Why?" she asked. "Mary-Kate, there's something you haven't told me....What is it? Tell me."

Gulp. She had me!

Chapter 2

I had no choice. I had to tell my sister the truth.

"I wrote postcards to our friends back home," I told Ashley. "I kind of said that we were working on our second mystery. A really big case."

"You lied?" Ashley stared at me.

"It's not a lie," I told her. "I have a hunch that we *will* solve a case on this cruise!"

"But what if we don't?" Ashley asked. "Then what will you tell our friends?"

"I don't know," I said.

I felt awful. What would I tell Brighton? And Cara and Vanessa? Our three best friends would never believe me about anything again.

Ashley shook her head at me. "Mary-Kate, you're always getting carried away!"

"I know," I said. I gazed across the deck. "Hey, there's Dad," I said. "Over there by the pool. Let's talk to him. Maybe he can help."

We headed that way.

Dad sat in a lounge chair. He was typing away on his laptop computer. He looked up as we walked over to his chair.

"Hi, spies," he called. "Good news! I'm almost finished with the dolphin program."

Dad was working on a special computer program. It would help people communicate information to the dolphins.

Our mom and dad are computer geniuses. People hire them to write special computer programs. They travel all over the world solving important problems. Of course, solving computer problems isn't nearly as exciting as solving mysteries. Still, the dolphin program was pretty cool.

Just then Mom rushed up to us. "There you all are," she said. Mom pointed her finger at Dad's computer. "No more working, Jack! We're on vacation, remember?"

"I was just making some notes, Terri," he told her with a smile.

"And what about you two?" Mom asked Ashley and me. "You took off after breakfast without telling anyone where you were going—again."

"Guilty," I said.

"*With* an explanation," Ashley added. "We were looking for work."

"No!" Dad gasped. He pretended to be horrified. "No work on vacation!"

Mom laughed. "Maybe I should hire you girls. You could help me keep track of my twin daughters," she teased.

Hmmm. "It's a weird idea, but it *would* be

a case—" I started to say.

Ashley poked me. Hard. "Mom is kidding, Mary-Kate!" Ashley exclaimed.

"But Mom is also right," Dad added. He put his computer into its shiny metal case and shut the lid. "We are on this cruise to relax. So no more work today."

Just then a chubby man stumbled by. He was wearing a brightly colored shirt. It was Mr. Kramer.

Mr. Kramer is the manager of Sea World. Sea World is a marine-life park filled with dolphins, whales, birds, and fish. Mr. Kramer hired Mom and Dad to write a computer program for the dolphins at Sea World. He was also a good friend. He had arranged this trip for us. He knew Mom and Dad were working too hard and needed a rest.

"Mr. Kramer, this cruise is wonderful," Mom said.

"I'm glad you're having a good time," Mr.

Kramer said. He tried to smile. But his big brown mustache drooped. A strange expression crossed his face.

"Mr. Kramer, you don't look so good," I said.

"I'm seasick," moaned Mr. Kramer. "I forgot that I get seasick—even in a bathtub! Excuse me—" Mr. Kramer dashed away.

"I can't believe that the head of Sea World is seasick!" I said.

"I hope he feels better soon," Mom said. She turned toward Dad. "Let's put the computer in our cabin. I could use a swim."

"Great idea," Dad replied. "Coming, girls?"

I spotted a tall man coming our way. He was wearing a white cap and a jacket with gold buttons. The captain of the ship!

"Uh, we have something else to do," I told them. Our parents strolled away.

I poked Ashley. "There's the captain," I told her. "Let's give him one of our business cards! If anyone knows what's happening on this ship, he does!"

Ashley and I rushed over to the captain.

"Excuse me, Captain, sir," I began.

He looked at me. He looked at Ashley. He shook his head and rubbed his eyes.

"I'm seeing double!" he joked.

Ashley and I groaned. People were always making that dumb joke. It's one of the annoying things about being a twin.

"You're seeing fine," I said politely. I handed the captain a business card. "You just happen to have twin detectives on board."

"The Trenchcoat Twins," Ashley added.

"Then all we need is a mystery," the captain said. He gave us a serious look. "Actually there *is* something missing. Could you find it for me?" he asked.

Ashley drew in a deep breath. I felt my heart beat faster. At last! The mystery we were waiting for!

Chapter 3

I whipped out my detective's notebook. I keep it with me at all times. (Great-grandma Olive told me to do that. Because a detective never knows when an important clue will show up.) Ashley handed me a pen. I was ready to write.

"What's missing, Captain?" I asked.

"Tell us all the details," Ashley added.

"My glasses are gone," the captain said.

I rolled my eyes and pointed to the captain's chest. "Uh—your glasses are hanging around your neck," I told him.

"They are?" The captain patted his chest. He felt his glasses. He blushed and put them on.

"Ah!" he said. "Thank you very much, girls. Good detective work!" He waved goodbye and walked away.

Ashley looked at me. "Some case," she teased.

I groaned. "Lost glasses! I can hardly write home about *that*!" I leaned against the railing. "I'm starting to get worried, Ashley," I said. "Really worried."

I wished I was at home. I missed our dog, Clue. Clue is our silent partner. She's a brown and white Basset Hound with floppy ears and a big wet nose—a big help in sniffing out clues. Dogs aren't allowed on the cruise ship. Which is too bad. I bet Clue would have sniffed out a case in a second.

I stared down at the pool deck below. Ashley stood next to me.

Suddenly she giggled. "Look, Mary-Kate," she said. "It's Bobo and Flippy!"

Bobo and Flippy are two guys who dress

like clowns. They usually hang out at Sea World. They wear black pants and shirts, black hats, and white cotton gloves. They cover their faces with white face paint. And they never talk. Instead they act out everything they want to say.

They make everyone laugh. Mr. Kramer liked them so much that he had asked them to come on vacation with us.

"Look at those silly clowns," Ashley said. "What are they doing now?"

Bobo pretended to squirt Flippy with slimy suntan lotion. Flippy pretended to squirt Bobo. Then both of them pretended to slip and slide in puddles of lotion.

Bobo waved his arms around and fell on top of Flippy. Flippy didn't move. Bobo leaned close to him. He was making sure that Flippy was all right. Suddenly Flippy squirted pretend lotion right in Bobo's face!

Ashley and I laughed and clapped. So did

the people on the deck below.

"Look, Mary-Kate, there's Mom and Dad!" Ashley pointed at the bright blue swimming pool. Mom's hot-pink bathing suit was easy to spot in the water.

"The pool looks great! It's really hot out," Ashley said. "I'm going swimming."

"Wait, Ashley!" I said. "What about finding a mystery? I'm desperate!"

"Why don't you just write our friends new postcards?" she said. "Tell them you'll let them know as soon as you have a *real* case. All right, Mary-Kate?" she asked.

"All right," I grumbled.

"Well, I'm going to change into my bathing suit," Ashley said. She hurried away.

"Wait up, Ashley!" I hurried after her.

Trenchcoat Twins should always stick together. Besides, I'd rather go swimming *now*. And maybe write those postcards *later*.

The passenger cabins were a couple

decks below. The ship had many elevators to travel from deck to deck. The elevators were made of clear glass. They were so cool!

The elevator doors opened. Ashley and I stepped inside. I pressed the button for the veranda deck, and we rode down.

"Last one in our room is a rotten private eye!" Ashley yelled. We raced each other down the hall.

Ashley won. Just my luck. I put my key into the lock.

KA-THUMP!

I grabbed Ashley's arm. "Shh!" I leaned closer to our door. "What was that sound?"

"I didn't hear anything—" Ashley started to say.

KA-THUMP!

"I heard it that time," Ashley whispered.

The noise came from inside our room. I pulled the key out of the lock. "If Mom and Dad are at the pool—" I began.

"And you and I are out here—" Ashley continued.

"Then who's making that noise in our room?" I finished.

GULP! We ran around a corner. We stood with our backs pressed against the wall.

I glanced at my watch—it was 10:14 A.M. I wrote the time in my detective's notebook. Then I heard our cabin door open and close. I heard footsteps rushing down the hall.

"Is it safe to look?" Ashley whispered.

"We have to!" I whispered back.

Ashley and I peeked around the corner. I saw a man's back. He was sneaking away. He clutched a shiny metal suitcase.

"That's Dad's computer case!" I said.

"Who would want to steal *that*?" Ashley asked.

The man stopped. He glanced over his shoulder. We both saw his face.

It was Mr. Kramer!

Chapter 4

Mr. Kramer ran down the hall and disappeared around another corner.

"Quick! After him!" I shouted.

Ashley and I raced after Mr. Kramer. We turned the corner. The hallway was empty.

"We lost him," Ashley said.

"I can't believe Mr. Kramer stole Dad's computer," I said.

We had a mystery.

I wouldn't have to write *any* postcards now. I should have been happy. I should have been excited.

But this was one crime that *wasn't* going to be fun to solve. Because we already knew who the thief was.

And he was our friend.

"We'd better go tell Mom and Dad," I said.

We ran back up to the pool deck. Our parents were still in the pool.

"Mom! Dad!" I yelled.

They climbed out of the pool and hurried over to us.

"What's wrong?" Mom asked.

"We found a crime," I told them.

"But it's already solved," Ashley said.

Mom and Dad both looked surprised. I told them about the stolen computer.

"Mr. Kramer? A thief? It can't be," Dad said. "Why would he take our computer?"

"Mr. Kramer hired us to write the dolphin program," Mom added. "He doesn't need to steal it. It doesn't make any sense."

Sometimes Mom sounds just like Ashley!

"We don't know why he did it," Ashley said. "But we saw him, Mom."

"And he was being very sneaky," I said. "Please. You've got to believe us!"

Mom and Dad exchanged a look. "I guess we should check this out," Dad said.

We all hurried back to our cabin. Dad went over to the table where he usually worked. "The computer was right here," he said. He searched through the rest of the cabin—from top to bottom.

"It's all gone," he said angrily. "The computer, the disk—the whole dolphin program!"

"But it's okay, Dad," I told him. "All we have to do is find Mr. Kramer. We'll make him give it back," I said.

Dad frowned. "It wouldn't hurt to talk to him. Maybe he can explain what's going on," he said.

We took the elevator down to Mr. Kramer's cabin. Dad knocked. Mr. Kramer answered the door, wearing his pajamas.

I whipped out my trusty notebook. "Mr. Kramer, where were you at 10:14 A.M.?"

Mr. Kramer seemed startled. "I was in the bathroom. Being sick," he answered. "I haven't left this room all morning."

"Can you prove that?" I asked. I held my breath.

"No." Mr. Kramer said. His face suddenly looked green. "Oooh," he moaned. "I think I'm going to be sick again!" He shut the door.

Dad sighed. "Mr. Kramer didn't leave his cabin. He's too sick."

"But we *saw* him. Mr. Kramer *is* the thief," Ashley said.

"You *thought* you saw him," Mom said.

"We'd better tell a security officer about this," Dad added.

"Your father's right. Let the grown-ups take care of this," Mom told us. She and Dad hurried away.

Ashley turned to me. "Let the grown-ups take over?" she asked.

We looked at each other. "No way!" we said together.

"I know we can solve this case, Ashley," I said. "It will be so easy. We saw the thief taking the computer. Now all we have to do is prove it!"

Chapter 5

I took out my detective notebook and began to write.

CRIME: Stolen computer. TIME: 10:14 A.M. CLUE: We saw the thief. SUSPECT: Mr. Kramer.

I looked up at Ashley. "We need some evidence. Let's search for some clues," I said.

"We should start by searching for fingerprints," Ashley said. "Everyone's fingerprints are different. We might find Mr. Kramer's fingerprints in our cabin. That would be proof that he's the thief."

I nodded. "Ready, Detective Olsen?"

"Ready, Detective Olsen," Ashley replied.

I reached under our bunk bed and pulled

out a purple backpack. I opened the back-pack and took out a bottle of white powder.

"Fingerprinting powder ready," I said.

Our great-grandmother Olive sent us the fingerprinting kit. She also sent a book that taught us everything we needed to know about fingerprints.

Now we knew that fingerprints are patterns on your skin. They are made up of curvy lines. Skin is normally very sticky. When you touch something, it usually leaves a fingerprint behind.

Ashley reached into the backpack and took out a small round brush. "Fingerprinting brush ready," she said.

I sprinkled the white powder on the table where Dad used the computer. Ashley swept the brush across the powder. Most of the powder came off.

"Aha! Here's one!" Ashley said.

She pointed to a blurry spot on the table.

The white powder stuck to the curvy lines of the fingerprint. Ashley lifted her magnifying glass. "Time for a closer look," she said.

The magnifying glass made the fingerprint seem really big.

"I can see the lines perfectly," she said.

"Here's the fingerprint file," I said. I pulled some pieces of cardboard out of the backpack.

We had a pretty big fingerprint file. It was made up of more than a dozen cards. The cards had all of our family's fingerprints on them. And the prints of all of our friends. We even had Clue's paw prints!

I sifted through the file and pulled out cards for Mom, Dad, Ashley and me. I held up the first card. It had Dad's fingerprints on it. Ashley and I peered at the print on the table. The pattern of lines on the fingerprint was different from Dad's fingerprints.

"This isn't Dad's," Ashley said.

Next I held up the card with Ashley's fingerprints. The lines on the card matched it perfectly.

"It's *your* fingerprint, Ashley." I sighed.

"We'll try again," Ashley said.

She brushed the table with white powder again. "I found two more fingerprints!"

We studied the second fingerprint.

"This one is mine," I said.

We both stared at the third fingerprint. It had a strange pattern of curvy loops. We studied our fingerprint cards. It wasn't mine or Ashley's. It wasn't Mom's or Dad's.

"This isn't one of ours," I said.

Ashley's eyes widened. "We've got to know if this print belongs to Mr. Kramer."

"Right," I said. "And there's only one way to find out!"

Chapter 6

"We have to get Mr. Kramer's fingerprints. And we should take this fingerprint along—as evidence," Ashley said.

She put a piece of tape over the strange fingerprint. The white powder stuck to the tape. Now we could take the fingerprint with us.

I helped Ashley wipe the powder off the table. Mom would be mad if we made a mess. We were always careful to keep our detective work neat and clean. Great-grandma Olive said a good detective does her job and leaves nothing behind.

I slipped the fingerprinting kit back into

our purple backpack.

"Now let's go see if Mr. Kramer's fingerprints match this one," Ashley said.

We checked out Mr. Kramer's cabin first. Ashley knocked. Nobody answered.

"Try the door. If it's open, we can get inside and check things out," I said.

Ashley tried the doorknob. "Locked," she told me.

I tried the doorknob, too. *Definitely* locked.

"Well, we can't get Mr. Kramer's fingerprints from his cabin. How about from his doorknob?" I asked.

"Uh, Mary-Kate—now *our* fingerprints are all over the doorknob," Ashley reminded me.

Oops.

"Then we'll just have to find Mr. Kramer," Ashley said.

We searched the rest of the cabin decks. No Mr. Kramer. We went up one deck. We searched a huge empty ballroom where fancy lights hung from the ceiling. No Mr. Kramer.

We searched the empty dining room. Ashley made us check everywhere—even under the tables! Sometimes I think she's *too* good a detective!

But there was still no Mr. Kramer.

Finally we rode the elevator up to the main deck.

"Look! There he is!" Ashley exclaimed.

Mr. Kramer was stretched out in a deck chair. His eyes were closed. There was no one sitting around him.

Ashley crept into the row of chairs behind his. I followed her.

Zzzzuuuhhh!

"He's asleep! And snoring really loud," I whispered. "No wonder nobody's sitting near him."

"Let's get started," Ashley said. She

opened the purple backpack and pulled out a black ink pad. She handed it to me. She took out a blank piece of cardboard.

"You ink his fingers," she ordered.

How could Ashley be so calm at a time like this? What if Mr. Kramer woke up?

I held my breath and tiptoed closer.

I lifted one of Mr. Kramer's hands. It felt heavy—and very clammy. He really *was* sick.

"Yuck!" I said. Mr. Kramer's mustache twitched.

"Shhhh!" Ashley hissed at me.

Mr. Kramer kept snoring. I placed his hand onto the ink pad and pressed down. Now Mr. Kramer had ink on all his fingers. Ashley slipped the blank piece of cardboard under his hand.

"Now," she whispered.

I pressed down on Mr. Kramer's inky fingers for three seconds. When I lifted his hand, there were five black fingerprints left on the cardboard. Perfect!

The snoring stopped. Mr. Kramer's mustache wiggled.

"He's waking up!" Ashley whispered.

"Yikes!" I dropped Mr. Kramer's hand. "Run!" I cried.

I ran. Ashley ran beside me.

"Aaaahhh!" Mr. Kramer groaned as he woke up. He stretched and rubbed his eyes.

I glanced over my shoulder. And laughed out loud.

Mr. Kramer's fingers spread wide black streaks of ink all over his face!

"Wait till he looks in a mirror," I said to Ashley. "Is *he* going to be surprised!"

Chapter 7

"Mary-Kate, come quick!" Ashley said.

We were sitting at a table in the ship's huge dining room. It was a few minutes before lunch. We had the whole place to ourselves.

"Look at these fingerprints," Ashley told me. She handed me the magnifying glass.

I studied the prints we had taken from Mr. Kramer. "But Mr. Kramer's prints *don't* match the one we found on the table in our cabin!"

"And that means he *didn't* take the computer!" Ashley exclaimed.

"But we *saw* him." I said, puzzled.

"Fingerprints never lie." Ashley said. "So if

Mr. Kramer didn't do it..."

"Then who did?" I interrupted.

I peered at the fingerprint's curvy loops. We had to find out who it belonged to.

"This doesn't make sense. Unless there are *two* Mr. Kramers," I said.

"Two people who look exactly alike? How could that be?" Ashley asked.

I pointed at the mirror beside the table. Our two faces stared back at us. They looked exactly alike.

"I rest my case," I said. "We look exactly alike."

"So, you think Mr. Kramer has a twin?" Ashley asked. She seemed doubtful.

"No," I replied, "not a twin. If he had a twin, I guess we would have met him. But there could be someone on the ship who looks just like him."

Mom and Dad came in for lunch. We told them our idea about the two Mr. Kramers.

"Strange idea. But I suppose it's possible," Mom said.

"But there are hundreds of passengers on the ship. How will you find someone who looks like Mr. Kramer?" Dad asked.

"Don't worry," Ashley told him.

I grinned. "We have a plan!"

We're Mary-Kate and Ashley—the Trenchcoat Twins! There we were—on a family cruise.

And so was Mr. Kramer. He was Mom and Dad's boss at Sea World.

Even our friends Bobo and Flippy were on the cruise.

Ashley and I thought the cruise was almost perfect—if only we had a case to crack.

We asked everybody on the ship for a mystery to solve—but no luck!

Until we spotted a man stealing Dad's computer case. The man looked just like Mr. Kramer!

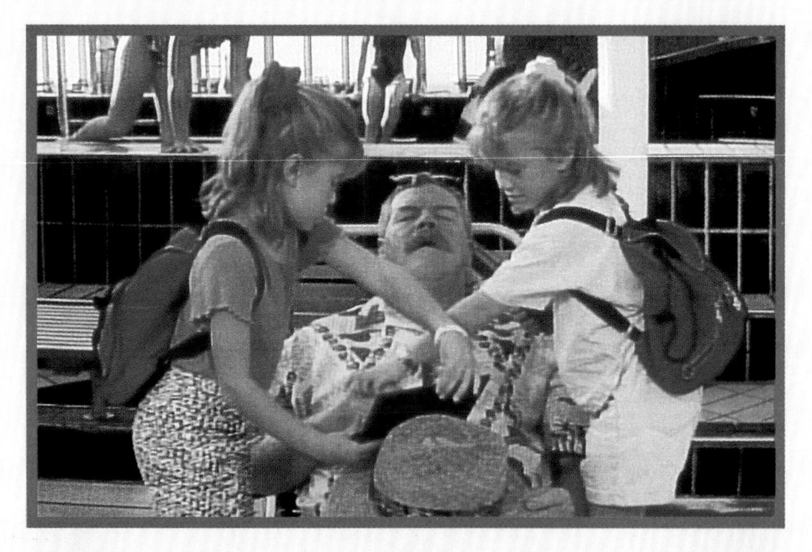

While Mr. Kramer was napping, we took his fingerprints.

But the fingerprints didn't match the ones we found in Mom and Dad's cabin!

Time for fun! Ashley and I sang and danced with Bobo and Flippy in the ship's talent show!

After our act, we found the missing computer case!

But then the computer case was stolen by Mr. Kramer again!

What was going on? Now there were two Mr. Kramers fighting over the case!

Were the two Mr. Kramers twins? Or was this one wearing a mask? Nope!

But the other one was!

Oh, wow! The fake Mr. Kramer was Bobo!

But why did Bobo try to steal Dad's computer case? Ashley and I figured it out—can you?

Chapter 8

Ashley and I quickly ate lunch. Then we hurried off to find Bobo and Flippy. We found them in the ship's theater.

There was going to be a big talent show today. Bobo and Flippy were in it. They love to perform as much as I do.

"Hi, guys. Ashley and I have a favor to ask you," I said.

"We'd like to be in the ship's talent show with you," Ashley told them.

Bobo and Flippy jumped in the air and clapped.

"We have an idea for a very special song," Ashley said. "We're going to pretend to be all kinds of different people."

"Will you help us?" I asked.

Bobo and Flippy nodded.

Ashley and I sang our song through twice for Bobo and Flippy. Then they showed us where the dressing room was. We went inside and changed into special costumes.

We both wore striped sailor shirts with white pants. My shirt had blue and white stripes. Ashley's shirt had red and white stripes. We both wore white sailor hats.

"This is going to be fun!" Ashley said. She straightened her hat. She tightened her pig-tails. I tightened mine.

"Do you have the surprise?" Ashley asked.

I checked my pockets. "Surprise in place."

"Then Olsen and Olsen are on the case," Ashley said.

We went to find Bobo and Flippy. They were in their dressing room down the hall.

Flippy blew us a kiss. He pretended to

pick flowers. He tossed a make-believe flower to each of us.

"Thanks, Flippy," I said.

The band began to play our music. "We're on!" Ashley said.

We ran out onstage. Bobo and Flippy ran on after us. I spotted Mom and Dad in the front row of the audience. They smiled and waved as Ashley and I sang this song:

"What if a magic genie said to you:
You can be anyone you want.
Now tell me who.
Anybody? Anybody!
Think it through!
Who would you be?
Who would you be?
Choose your identity.
Race-car driver?
Deep-sea diver?
Who would you be?"

Bobo and Flippy acted out the parts of the characters in the song.

First they pretended to be superheroes. Bobo whipped out a cape and pretended to fly through the air. Flippy pretended to be superstrong. He lifted a set of enormous weights. (We knew the weights were phoney. They weighed hardly anything!)

Everyone in the audience laughed.

Then the two clowns pretended to be fashion models. They stood on their tiptoes and pranced across the stage. They swung their heads as if they had long, flowing hair.

The audience clapped and laughed even louder. Bobo and Flippy pretended to be musicians next. They leaped off the stage and ran up to the real musicians.

Bobo took away the trumpet player's horn and pretended to blow hard. No sound came out. Flippy shook his head at Bobo. He pulled a set of drumsticks away from the drummer. Flippy pretended to play the drums on Bobo's back. This time, the *real* drummer played along.

Flippy jumped back in shock. Everyone was laughing and clapping and having a great time.

"Get ready for the surprise," I whispered to Ashley.

I reached into my pockets and took out—two mustaches!

Two big brown mustaches. Just like Mr. Kramer's.

"Remember the plan," Ashley whispered. "The thief had a mustache and looked just like Mr. Kramer. So we'll hold a mustache right under the nose of every person in the audience."

I nodded. "Right. The mustache will make someone look like Mr. Kramer. And then we'll know who the thief is!"

Chapter 9

Ashley and I hurried through the audience. We held the mustache under every nose as we sang:

"Who would you be?
Choose your identity."

Ashley covered the left side of the audience. I went to the right. I held my mustache up to a thin man. He didn't look at all like Mr. Kramer. I rushed up to a very heavy lady. Nope. She didn't look like Mr. Kramer either.

I glanced at Ashley. She was holding the

mustache under the nose of a squirming two-year-old. Like I said, sometimes Ashley is *too* good a detective!

The song was over. Ashley and I had looked at every nose.

Nobody looked like Mr. Kramer!

We didn't find the thief.

Bobo and Flippy bowed. Ashley and I smiled and waved at the audience. Mom blew us a kiss from the front row. Dad gave us a thumbs-up sign as we ran offstage. Then the next person in the talent show started singing.

Ashley and I ran back to our dressing room. We sat in front of the mirror. It was surrounded with bright, round light bulbs. It would have been fun to sit there and pretend we were movie stars—if we didn't have a case to crack!

"Now what? Nobody looked like Mr. Kramer," I said. I took out my pigtails and combed my hair smooth again.

"Maybe the thief *doesn't* look anything like Mr. Kramer," Ashley said.

Now I was really confused. "How could that be?" I asked.

"He might be an expert at changing his looks. He could have worn a disguise. Not just a fake mustache," she said.

Ashley was right!

Hmmm.

"But how do we find the Mr. Kramer who *isn't* Mr. Kramer? The one who's wearing the disguise?" I asked my sister.

"Uh—I have no idea," Ashley said.

"Great. We have no suspects. And no more clues." I sighed.

What would Great-grandma Olive do in a case like this? I wondered.

"Great-grandma Olive always says, 'don't give up,'" Ashley told me. "'If you're stuck, review the clues.'"

I looked at my twin in surprise. Sometimes I think she can read my mind!

I pulled out my notebook and read through my notes again. It didn't help at all. I didn't have a single hunch left!

"Well, we'll have to find new suspects and new clues. And fast!" Ashley said.

Right again! "What are we waiting for?" I asked.

Ashley and I hurried out of the theater. We searched everywhere for a Mr. Kramer—the real one *or* the one in the disguise.

No luck.

We entered the part of the ship where people went shopping. It was a big, huge covered deck. Stores lined both sides of the deck, just like in a regular shopping mall.

It was jammed full of people.

"Don't look now. But Mr. Kramer's sitting on a bench behind you," I told Ashley.

Yes!

We ducked down behind a low wall. It held planters that were filled with palm trees and brightly colored flowers. Ashley peeked through the leaves of the plants.

This Mr. Kramer didn't have smears of ink on his cheeks.

"He washed his face since the last time we saw him!" Ashley grinned.

Then the smile disappeared from her face. "Unless—"

I stared at my sister. "Unless this is the *fake* Mr. Kramer," I said. "And *he* never had ink on his face!"

"Think fast," Ashley told me. "What should we do?"

Before I could answer I saw a lady in a pink sundress walk up to Mr. Kramer. They started talking.

"Haven't we seen her somewhere before?" Ashley asked.

"She does look familiar," I said.

Suddenly I knew where we had seen her.

"Ashley!" I cried. "It's the lady who was sitting next to the poodle! The one with the shifty eyes."

Mr. Kramer reached under the bench and pulled out a metal case. The lady grabbed the metal case. She hurried away.

"Ashley! Did you see that?"

It was Dad's computer case!

Chapter 10

"Let's go, Ashley!" I shouted. "She's getting away with Dad's computer!"

Ashley and I ran after the woman holding the metal case. She walked quickly across the shopping area. She disappeared inside a dress store. We followed.

It was a small store. The shopkeeper turned and stared at Ashley and me. She was a short woman with curly black hair.

Ashley gave her a friendly smile. "Good afternoon!" she said.

"Um, we're looking for a present for our mother," I told her.

"Your mother is lucky. Let me know if

you need help." The shopkeeper smiled back and went on with her work.

We walked around the room. We pretended to look at dresses and blouses. We were really looking for the woman in the pink sundress. But there was no sign of her.

"Mary-Kate, over here!" Ashley pointed to the dressing rooms.

Some long dresses hung on a peg on a dressing room door. The dresses reached almost to the floor. The metal case peeked out from underneath them.

"Dad's computer!" Ashley whispered.

Ashley and I crept down the hall.

"Be careful," Ashley said.

I stooped down and grabbed the metal case. "Got it!" I whispered.

Yap-yap-yap! Yap-yap-yap!

I glanced down. I realized that the case was a funny size. And the back of it was made out of wires. The woman's poodle was inside! He bared his teeth at me and started barking even louder.

"Uh-oh, Ashley. Mr. Kramer didn't give the lady Dad's computer case. He gave her a dog carrier—with a poodle inside!" I said.

"Then I guess this lady isn't the thief," Ashley said.

I groaned. "Talk about barking up the wrong tree!"

The dressing-room door started to open.

"Who's there?" the woman in the pink dress called out.

"No one!" I yelled.

I quickly put the dog carrier back on the ground. I grabbed Ashley's hand and pulled her out of the store. My heart was pounding hard.

"Look, Ashley—Mr. Kramer's still sitting on the bench," I said.

"We still have to find out if he's the *real* Mr. Kramer. But how?" Ashley asked.

"I have an idea. Let me do the talking," I told her.

We hurried over to Mr. Kramer. I gave him a big, friendly smile. "Hi there, Mr. Kramer!"

Mr. Kramer smiled back. "Hello, Mary-Kate—or Ashley. Which twin are you?"

"I could ask you the same question," I blurted. Ashley jabbed me in the ribs.

"Uh, I'm Mary-Kate," I said.

Sometimes I get really tired of answering that question. Telling people who I am is one of the boring parts of being a twin.

Ashley sat beside Mr. Kramer on the bench. "You don't look sick anymore, Mr. Kramer," she said. "You *were* sick this morning, weren't you?"

Mr. Kramer grinned. "Yes. But I feel a lot better now. I was watching that nice lady's poodle for her," he said.

"Let me handle this," I whispered to Ashley. Ashley is great at finding evidence.

But I'm much better at talking to people.

I turned back to Mr. Kramer.

"Mr. Kramer, since you're not sick anymore, you might be hungry for lunch. But I can't remember all the things you like on a hot dog. Could you tell me again?"

Ashley and I ate lunch with Mr. Kramer almost every day at Sea World. I always order the extra ketchup and mustard. Ashley likes plenty of relish. But Mr. Kramer orders his hot dogs the most unusual way of all.

Mr. Kramer gave me a funny look. "It's nice of you to ask, Mary-Kate. But I couldn't eat a hot dog right now. Thanks anyway."

"But Mr. Kramer, what if we really wanted to get you a hot dog? How would you like it?" I tried again.

Mr. Kramer sighed. "Mary-Kate, you know very well that I don't like *anything* at all on my hot dogs."

Yes! Ashley and I slapped a high five.

"You're the *real* Mr. Kramer, all right," I said. Then I quickly explained how Dad's computer case was stolen.

"But now we know that *you* didn't steal it," Ashley said.

"I'm sorry we had to question you," I added.

"I understand," Mr. Kramer told us. "But I'm glad you girls are on the case. Good luck finding the thief," he added.

"Thanks," I said. We waved good-bye to Mr. Kramer and hurried toward the elevators.

On the way we passed the grown-ups' game room.

It was filled with tables. People sat at the tables playing games. Some of them were playing cards.

"Let's go, Mary-Kate. Dad's computer case isn't in the game room," Ashley told me.

"Wait a minute. What is Flippy doing in here?" I asked.

"Acting silly, as usual," Ashley answered.

We watched as Flippy leaned over one of the tables. He pretended to roll dice. He pretended he was winning—big time.

He leaped up and did a cartwheel. Then he pretended to stuff his pockets with lots of prizes. Everyone around him laughed.

"And there's Bobo, too. But he's not being very silly," Ashley said. She stared at Bobo.

Bobo stood at another table. He wasn't doing cartwheels. He wasn't leaping into the air. He wasn't pretending to win prizes.

Bobo leaned over a table. He placed some real money on the table. Real sweat rolled down his face.

Bobo lost the game—he lost all his money!

Bobo began to cry real tears.

"Something is very wrong," I said to Ashley. "He's really crying. Clowns never do anything for real!"

Chapter 11

"Ashley, I have a terrible hunch." I stared at my twin.

"You and your hunches! Try to be calm and logical for once," Ashley said.

I took out my detective's notebook. "No way. You be logical. I'll write down everything you say."

Ashley nodded. "Then write this: PLACE: Game room. CLUE: Bobo is playing a game for *real*—and losing his money. OTHER CLUE: Bobo knows all about disguises. DEDUCTION—"

"DEDUCTION: Bobo is our new suspect," I finished.

"We'd better take Bobo's fingerprints. If

they match the one on the table, then he's the thief," Ashley said.

"Let's check Bobo's dressing room," I said.

We hurried back to the theater, where the talent show was still going on. We went backstage and headed to the dressing rooms.

The door to Bobo and Flippy's room was open. We quickly went inside. I opened the purple backpack.

"Hurry! Bobo and Flippy might be back any minute," Ashley whispered.

I spread the white powder over their dressing table. Ashley pulled out the magnifying glass.

Suddenly we heard a loud knock at the door.

Yikes!

"Bobo? Flippy?" someone called. "Are you in there?"

Ashley and I dived into the open closet. Ashley crouched down. I squeezed in next to her. (Closets on a ship are very, very small.)

I pulled the closet door shut. It was dark. Hiding in closets and under beds is one of the worst parts of being a detective. Especially if you hate the dark. (I hate the dark.)

We both held our breath. We waited a minute or two. The room was quiet. Nobody came inside.

I peeked through a crack in the closet door.

"No one's there," I whispered. "Let's get out of this closet."

"Oops!" Ashley tripped over something lying on the floor of the closet. I helped her stand up. She had fallen over a small case. A metal case.

"Mary-Kate—look!" Ashley lifted the case.

I snapped it open.

Dad's computer was inside!

"The disks with the dolphin program are in the case, too!" Ashley said.

"Grab it!" I said.

Ashley and I raced out of the dressing room. We headed up the stairs to our cabin.

Oooff!

I bumped smack into Ashley. "Why did you stop?" I asked.

Ashley pointed to the top of the stairs. Mr. Kramer stood there. He was blocking the stairway.

"Look what we found, Mr. Kramer!" Ashley called.

Mr. Kramer growled. He didn't look as friendly as he did before. In fact, he didn't look friendly *at all.*

Gulp!

Mr. Kramer narrowed his eyes. Then he rushed down the stairs. He was heading right toward us!

Chapter 12

"Uh, Ashley—I think we just found the *fake* Mr. Kramer!" I said.

"Run!" Ashley screamed.

We turned and ran back down the stairs. The fake Mr. Kramer chased after us.

We headed toward the theater and raced through a side door. I pushed through a curtain. Ashley followed me.

We were onstage—again! Right in the middle of a group of dancers. There were a dozen men and women in a straight line across the stage. They were kicking their legs in time to the music.

"What do we do now?" I whispered.

"Dance!" Ashley whispered back.

She set the metal case down on the stage. Ashley and I kicked our legs. I tried to smile.

It was a good thing Ashley and I take dancing lessons at home. Ashley almost looked like part of the act. She had no trouble at all keeping up with the other dancers.

But I was having a hard time figuring out which leg to kick. I should have paid more attention in dancing class.

Mom and Dad were still in the audience. They were very surprised to see Ashley and me onstage again—dancing!

"Hey! My computer case!" Dad shouted.

"Mary-Kate!" Ashley shouted at the same time.

I whirled around. The fake Mr. Kramer was onstage. He grabbed the computer case and ran off.

"Stop that man!" shouted Dad.

He and Mom chased after Mr. Kramer.

Ashley and I followed. The audience laughed. They thought the whole thing was a funny act—part of the talent show!

The fake Mr. Kramer headed for the glass elevators. The doors slid open. He ducked inside.

The elevator doors slammed shut. The elevator began to rise. The fake Mr. Kramer waved good-bye through the glass. He laughed and twirled his phony mustache.

"Look, everyone!" Ashley shouted. She pointed to the other elevator. It was rising next to the fake Mr. Kramer's.

And inside it stood the real Mr. Kramer!

"There *are* two of them!" Mom said.

The two Mr. Kramers wore the same shirt and the same hat. They had the same face. But only one was the real Mr. Kramer.

The real Mr. Kramer turned and saw his twin in the elevator next to him. He also saw that the fake Mr. Kramer was carrying Dad's computer case. He shook his fist at the fake Mr. Kramer.

"We have to stop the thief!" I shouted.

Dad led us all into a third elevator. "Follow those elevators!" he said.

The first two elevators stopped at the sundeck. The fake Mr. Kramer jumped out and ran away. The real Mr. Kramer jumped out too and chased after him.

Then our elevator reached the sundeck. We jumped out—and ran into both Mr. Kramers fighting over the case.

Two security guards pulled them apart.

The captain walked up to us. He stared at Ashley and me. "Well, well." The captain chuckled. "Twin detectives—hot on the trail of twin suspects!"

"They're not suspects anymore. One of them is a thief," I said.

"This is our dad's computer. And *he* stole it!" Ashley pointed at the fake Mr. Kramer.

"But who *is* the thief?" the real Mr. Kramer asked.

I reached up and tugged at the fake Mr. Kramer's face.

It wasn't a face at all. It was a mask. And Ashley and I knew who was under the mask.

Someone who knew about Mom and Dad's special dolphin program.

Someone who needed money.

Someone who had to wear a clever disguise so we wouldn't recognize him.

I gave an extra hard tug. The mask came off in my hands. Mom and Dad gasped.

They could see the real thief now.

"Bobo?" Mr. Kramer asked.

"Bobo!" Mom cried.

"Bobo," Ashley and I said together.

Bobo ducked his head. Real tears rolled down his cheeks.

"Why did you do it? Why did you take the computer?" Mr. Kramer asked Bobo.

"I know why." The captain stepped forward. "I've been watching Bobo," he said. "He was losing money and wanted to get rich quick. Your parents' computer program is worth a lot of money. Bobo was going to sell it," he explained.

The security officers led Bobo away.

"Poor Bobo," I said.

"How did you girls ever figure out that the fake Mr. Kramer was really Bobo?" Mom asked us.

"Well, we finally remembered something that Great-grandma Olive taught us," Ashley answered.

"She said it's the hardest thing about being a detective," I added.

"And what is it?" Mom asked.

"She said that sometimes you *can't* believe your own eyes!" I said.

"She was right in this case," Dad said.

"Dad, is there anything we can do for

Bobo?" Ashley asked.

"Yes, we can get help for him. We'll do everything we can for Bobo. After all, we're still his friends," Dad said.

"I'm glad," I told him.

"Me too," Ashley said.

Dad put an arm around Ashley and me. "Congratulations, Mary-Kate and Ashley. You've solved another mystery!"

"And it was a tough case, too," Mr. Kramer said.

"Just simple logic," Ashley told him.

"We figured the thief was someone who was a good actor and who knew a lot about costumes," I added.

"We put together all the clues and the evidence. And they added up to Bobo," Ashley finished.

"You did a great job," Mom said.

"No problem," I answered. "Double trouble is no trouble—for the Trenchcoat Twins!"

Chapter 13

"Did you see that? The dolphins jumped higher than they ever jumped before!" I said.

We were back at Sea World. The seats at Dolphin Stadium were filled. The audience cheered loudly as they watched the dolphins perform.

Ashley and I sat by the edge of the dolphin pool. Mom and Dad were next to us.

Dad worked at his computer. Mom wore a special set of headphones. She listened to the sounds the dolphins made under the water. She was recording the sounds.

Dad typed into the computer: *Dolphins, swim in a circle.*

The dolphins heard the signal. They swam in a circle. Then Dad typed: *Dolphins, swim fast.*

The dolphins swam very fast.

"The program is working better than ever," Dad said.

"Yes. And soon we'll be able to teach them more signals. Recording the dolphins helps us learn how they communicate," Mom said.

"Speaking of communicating," Ashley turned to me. "Did you ever write those postcards to our friends?" she asked.

"Yes. *After* we caught the real thief," I replied. "But don't worry, Ashley, I left out plenty of details. So you'll be able to tell Cara, Vanessa, and Brighton all about it yourself."

"And don't forget another person we need to tell," Ashley said.

"Who's that?" I asked.

Ashley grinned. "Great-grandma Olive!"

"She'll be the first to know," I said.

Yes! Ashley and I slapped a high five.

Dad typed another signal into his computer. "Here comes the big finish," he told us.

The dolphins soared up into the air. They spun around. Then they dived back into the water at the exact same time.

SPLASH!

The audience loved it! They clapped and cheered. So did Ashley and I.

Dad turned to us. "Our work at Sea World is finished—for now. We're going home," he said.

"I'll really miss Sea World," Ashley said. "It was so much fun!"

"Me too. But I'm glad we're going home," I said.

"How come?" Ashley asked.

"Because I have a hunch there's *another* mystery waiting there for two super-duper snoopers like us!"

Hi—from both of us!

Ashley and I loved our vacation on the cruise ship, but when it ended we were really glad to be going home. Mom and Dad said that was because we missed Trent and Lizzie—our older brother and little sister.

We said, "No way!" We wanted to get home because we had a hunch that there was a monster of a mystery waiting for us there. And we were right!

You can read all about it in *The Case Of The Fun House Mystery.* And, in the meantime, if you have any questions, you can write us at:

MARY-KATE & ASHLEY'S FUN CLUB™
859 HOLLYWOOD WAY, SUITE 412
BURBANK, CA 91505

We would love to hear from you!

Love
Mary-Kate and Ashley

It doesn't matter if you live around the corner...
or around the world...
If you are a fan of Mary-Kate and Ashley Olsen,
you should be a member of

MARY-KATE + ASHLEY'S FUN CLUB™

Here's what you get:
Our Funzine™
An autographed color photo
Two black & white individual photos
A full size color poster
An official **Fun Club™** membership card
A **Fun Club™** school folder
Two special **Fun Club™** surprises
A holiday card
Fun Club™ collectibles catalog
Plus a **Fun Club™** box to keep everything in

To join Mary-Kate + Ashley's Fun Club™, fill out the form below and send it along with

U.S. Residents – $17.00
Canadian Residents – $22 U.S. Funds
International Residents – $27 U.S. Funds

MARY-KATE + ASHLEY'S FUN CLUB™
859 HOLLYWOOD WAY, SUITE 275
BURBANK, CA 91505

NAME:____

ADDRESS:____

CITY:__________________STATE:__________ZIP:___________

PHONE: (____) _________________BIRTHDATE:____________

The party can't start without you...
You're Invited to Mary-Kate & Ashley's
with a shiny dolphin necklace!
Hawaiian Beach Party
with a beautiful keepsake locket!
Sleepover Party
Birthday Party
with a twin hearts necklace!
Christmas Party
with a snowflake necklace!
You've watched the videos, now read all the books! Order today!
❑ BCG93843-6 You're Invited to Mary-Kate & Ashley's Sleepover Party $12.95
❑ BCG88012-8 You're Invited to Mary-Kate & Ashley's Hawaiian Beach Party $12.95
❑ BCG76958-8 You're Invited to Mary-Kate & Ashley's Christmas Party $12.95
❑ BCG22593-6 You're Invited to Mary-Kate & Ashley's Birthday Party $12.95
Here's a message from Mary-Kate and Ashley...See you at the bookstore!
Available wherever you buy books, or use this order form
Scholastic Inc., P.O. Box 7502, 2931 East McCarty Street, Jefferson City, MO 65102
Please send me the books I have checked above. I am enclosing $_____ (please add $2.00 to cover shipping and handling). Send check or money order—no cash or C.O.D.s please.
Name
Birthdate
Address
City
State/Zip
Please allow four to six weeks for delivery. Offer good in U.S. only. Sorry, mail orders are not available to residents of Canada. Prices subject to change.
DUALSTAR PUBLICATIONS
PARACHUTE PRESS
SCHOLASTIC
YIT298

Join the Party!

Collect all three new videos from Mary-Kate & Ashley.